Norman Bethune

Terry Barber

MAPLE LEAF
SERIES

Norman Bethune is published by
Grass Roots Press, a division of Literacy Services of Canada Ltd.

PHONE 1–888–303–3213
WEBSITE www.grassrootsbooks.net

ACKNOWLEDGMENTS

We acknowledge the financial support of the Government of Canada through the Canada Book Fund (CBF) for our publishing activities.

Produced with the assistance of
the Government of Alberta, Alberta
Multimedia Development Fund.

**Government
of Alberta ■**

Editor: Dr. Pat Campbell
Image research: Dr. Pat Campbell
Book design: Lara Minja

Library and Archives Canada Cataloguing in Publication

Barber, Terry, date
        Norman Bethune / Terry Barber.

(Maple leaf series)
ISBN 978–1–926583–37–2

        1. Bethune, Norman, 1890–1939. 2. Surgeons—Canada—
Biography. 3. Surgeons—China—Biography. 4. Readers
for new literates. I. Title. II. Series: Barber, Terry, 1950– .
Maple leaf series.

PE1126.N43B36617 2011   428.6'2   C2011–905025–0

Printed in Canada

Contents

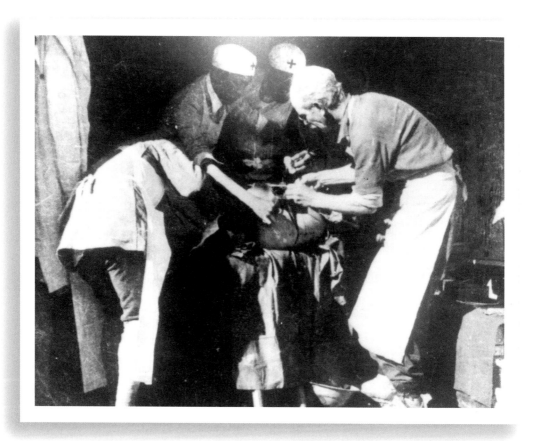

Dr. Norman Bethune saves a life.
1939

Norman Bethune

It is 1939. A soldier is dying. He has lost a lot of blood. A doctor rolls up his sleeve. The doctor removes his own blood. He transfers his blood to the soldier. The doctor is Norman Bethune.

Norman Bethune with his brother, mother, and sister.
1904

Early Years

Norman is born in 1890. His father is a minister. Norman does not want to follow in his father's footsteps. Norman wants to be a doctor. He does not want to save souls. He wants to save lives.

Norman is born in Ontario.

Norman at age 15.

Early Years

Norman starts university at the age of 19. He studies to be a doctor. He is a good student. But he thinks the courses are boring. After two years, Norman's money starts to run out. He must leave school to work.

Norman works at a lumber camp.
1911

Early Years

Norman works in camps in the bush. He works as a logger. He works with many men who cannot read or write. At night, Norman teaches these men in their shacks. Norman learns that life is hard for the working class.

Norman returns to university in 1912.

These men carry a hurt soldier.

World War I

Norman, age 25.

World War I starts in 1914. Norman joins the Army. He has one job. This job puts Norman's life at risk. Norman carries stretchers across the battlefield. Many soldiers bleed to death. They do not get the medical help they need.

Norman is sent to Belgium.

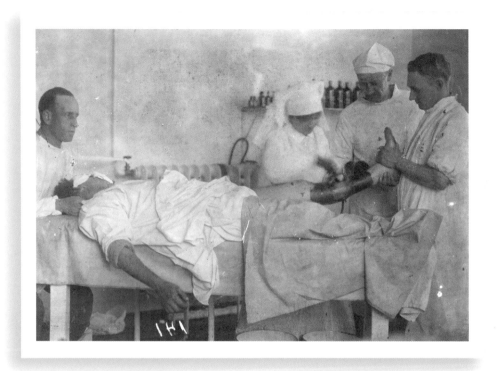

A medical team helps an injured soldier.

World War I

One day, Norman gets hurt. His left leg is ripped to the bone from **shrapnel**. He spends six months in the hospital. The hospitals are filled with soldiers. Norman sees so many people suffer.

Norman is released from the Army in 1915.

Norman Bethune gets his medical degree.

Norman Becomes Famous

Norman goes back to school in Canada. He gets his degree in 1916. But he does not stop learning. Norman moves to England. He takes special training. He becomes a chest and lung surgeon. He finds new ways to treat people.

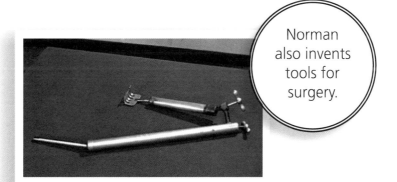

Norman also invents tools for surgery.

Norman and Frances marry in 1923.

Norman Becomes Famous

Norman works and plays hard. He attracts women like a magnet. He falls in love with a young woman from Scotland. Her name is Frances. On their wedding day, Norman says: "Now I can make your life a misery. But I will never bore you."

Norman and Frances divorce in 1927.

A free health clinic in the U.S.
1920

The Caring Doctor

Norman and Frances move to the U.S. Norman sets up his own health clinic. Norman works long hours. He charges a fee for his services. But he does not charge people who are poor. Some people give him food for his services.

The couple move to Detroit in 1924.

Norman gets better at a TB clinic.

The Caring Doctor

Norman works so hard. He almost works himself to death. Norman gets sick. He loses 23 kg. Norman has **TB** in his lungs. But Norman is lucky. He gets better. He has money to pay for health care.

TB stands for a disease called tuberculosis.

Norman operates on people with TB.

The Activist Doctor

Norman moves to Montreal in 1928.
He wants to change health care in
Canada. He wants everybody to
get health care at a fair price. The
Government of Canada does not start
a health care program. Norman feels
the government has no heart.

Norman
says, "The rich
man lives and
the poor man
dies."

Norman returns from the USSR.
1935

The Activist Doctor

Norman sails to the **USSR** in 1935.
The USSR has a **Communist** ruler.
Norman thinks the **Communist Party**
has changed the USSR for the better.
In the USSR, even poor people get free
health care. Norman wants Canada to
have better health care.

Norman
joins the
Communist Party
of Canada.

Norman stands in front of his mobile blood bank.

The Activist Doctor

In 1936, a **civil war** breaks out in
Spain. Norman goes to Spain. He
creates a **mobile** blood bank. People
from the city donate their blood.
Then Norman takes the blood to the
battlefields. Norman saves many lives.

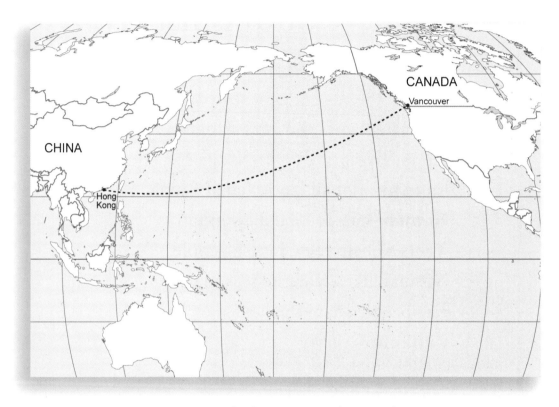

Norman sails from Canada to China.

1937

The Communist Doctor

It is 1937. Japan has **invaded** China. Norman sails to China. Norman wants to help the Chinese people. Norman likes what he sees in China. The people share the little they have with others.

World War II starts in 1939.

Norman Bethune meets with Mao Zedong.
1938

The Communist Doctor

Norman meets with Mao Zedong.
Mao is a communist. He is the leader
of China's Communist Party. They
talk about health care. They talk
about politics. Both like how the other
thinks.

Norman trains a man to be a doctor.

The Communist Doctor

China does not have enough doctors.
Norman sets up classes. He trains
people to be doctors and nurses.
Norman teaches basic medicine. The
new doctors and nurses work to save
lives. Norman works day and night.

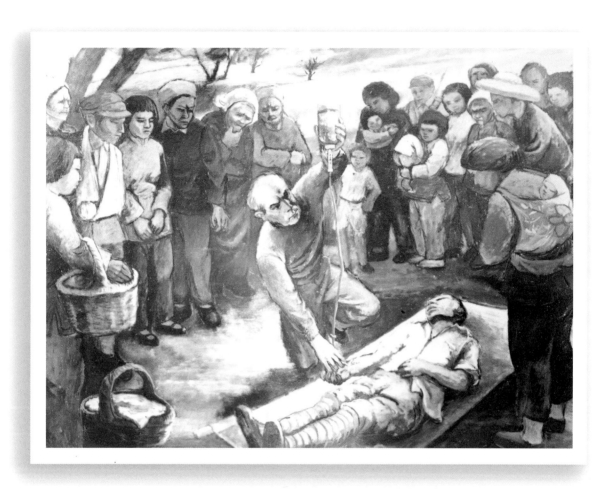

Norman gives blood to a patient.

Norman Becomes a Hero

The Chinese people see how hard Norman works. Norman shares his clothes. Norman shares his food. He even gives his blood to the wounded.

The Chinese people see Norman as a hero. Chinese soldiers have a battle cry: "Attack, Bethune is with us!"

Norman travels with the Chinese soldiers.

Norman Becomes a Hero

Norman believes doctors must go to the wounded. He travels long distances. He lives and works in bad conditions. At times, he lives in caves. Norman becomes weak and tired. He loses weight. But Norman is happy. He feels needed.

Norman walks more than 644 km (400 miles) to reach people.

Norman's body is carried to his grave.
1939

Norman Becomes a Hero

Norman cuts his finger as he operates. He gets a blood infection. He is too weak to fight off the infection. He gets very sick. Yet he keeps working. Norman dies on November 12, 1939. He is only 49 years old.

Mao Zedong writes a speech.

Norman Becomes a Hero

Mao hears of Norman's death. Mao writes a speech about Norman. People across China listen to the speech. Norman died to help China. China does not forget Norman. He lives forever in the hearts of the Chinese people.

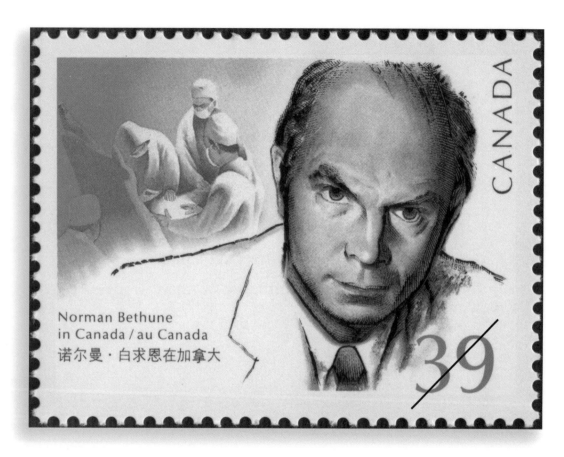

Norman Bethune
in Canada / au Canada
诺尔曼·白求恩在加拿大

CANADA

39

Canada Post makes a stamp in 1990.

Norman Becomes a Hero

Norman gets many honours in Canada and China. Both countries make stamps to honour Norman. Both countries build statues. In China, buildings are named after Norman. Norman helps to **unite** two countries.

Glossary

civil war: a war between two groups of people in the same country.

communist: a person who believes in communism.

Communist Party: a political party.

invade: to enter by force to conquer.

mobile: easily moved.

shrapnel: fragments from a shell or bomb.

TB: tuberculosis is a lung disease.

unite: to bring or join together.

USSR: Union of Soviet Socialist Republics.

Talking About the Book

What did you learn about Norman Bethune?

What words would you use to describe Norman?

Why did Norman want to change health care in Canada?

Do you think your country has a good health care program?

Norman worked as a doctor in many wars. Describe how he put his life at risk.

Why is Norman a hero in China?

Picture Credits